Good Night, World

by Nicola Edwards
Illustrated by Hannah Tolson

For Jack ~ N.E.   For Orton ~ H.T.

The pronunciations included in this book are supplied as a general guide only, as some languages featured vary in the way they are spoken around the world.

tiger tales

When the day is at an end, up to bed we'll go.
The sky becomes darker as the night begins to gro

hen the bright, golden sun sheds the last of its light,
we turn to each other and we say, "Good night!"

In Mandarin,
we say,
"Wǎn ān"
晚安
Wan-an

In a warm, bubbly bath, we build towers of foam.

Rubber duck bobs along as we sail our boat home.

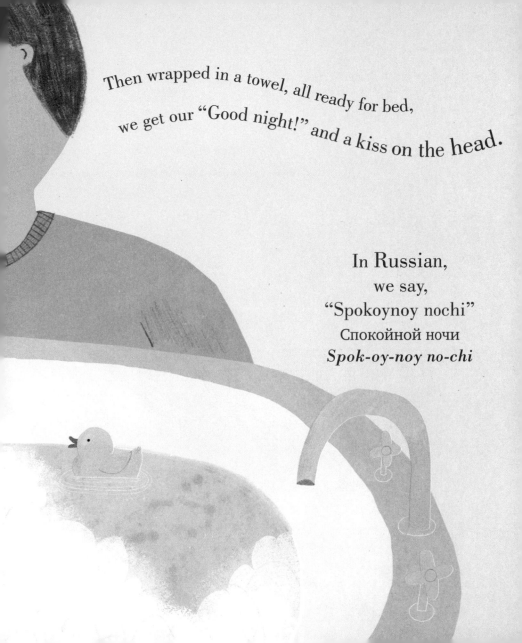

Then wrapped in a towel, all ready for bed,
we get our "Good night!" and a kiss on the head.

In Russian,
we say,
"Spokoynoy nochi"
Спокойной ночи
Spok-oy-noy no-chi

In front of the mirror,

we jostle for space.

We splish and we splash,

and we make it a race.

We wash up, then go out

and turn off the light.

We're ready for bed,

and we all say, "Good night!"

In Italian, we say,
"Buona notte"
Bwon-na no-tay

The teddies are tired, and the trains don't run late,

so the toys' next adventures will just have to wai

We clean our things up, make everything right

for more fun tomorrow. Until then, "Good night!"

In Finnish, we say,
"Hyvää yötä"
Hoo-vah ooh-er-tah

When we're far from our loved ones, and it's time for bed,
a phone call replaces a kiss on the head.

The voice says, "Good night!" and we don't feel so far.
Our "Good night!" finds you, too, wherever you are.

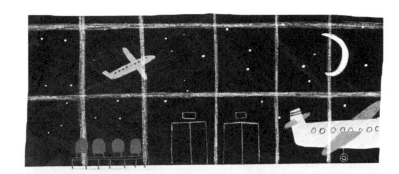

In Swahili, we say, "Usiku mwema"
Ooh-see-koo mweh-ma

When we're all here together,
we laugh and have fun,

telling jokes, sharing stories,
'til the long day is done.

nd soon it is time, so we turn off the light.

In a chorus of one voice, we all say, "Good night!"

In Spanish, we say,
"Buenas noches"
Bwen-oss no-chez

Tonight there's a tale

from a faraway place,

with pirates, a princess,

a journey to space · · ·

And slowly but surely

our eyes start to close.

We get our "Good night!"

and a kiss on the nose.

In Arabic, we say,
"Tisbah ala khair"
تصبح على خير
Tuss-bah el-la kher

When we've spent all our time
just running about,

and the day's wild adventures
have worn us right out,

we're carried to bed; we're already asleep.

We get a "Good night!" but we don't hear a peep.

In Hindi, we say, "Shubh raatri"
शुभरात्रि   *Shub raa-tree*

We doze in a tent by the light of the moon.

Trees rustle above us; we'll be fast asleep soon.

Under blankets of stars, we are snuggled in tight.

In the peace of our tent, we whisper, "Good night!"

In German, we say,
"Gute nacht"
Goo-teh naakt

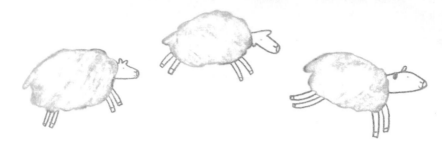

When those precious sweet dreams
just don't come right away,
like the Sandman got lost,
or his plan went astray,

if we can be patient
and count all those sheep,
before long, "Good night!"
will be followed by sleep.

In French, we say,
"Bonne nuit"
Bon nwee

Bedtime is something that everyone shares,

from children to chicks, and from bunnies to bears.

We all get tucked in, from the big to the small,

and say our good nights, one by one, each to all.

In Korean,
we say,
"Jal jayo"
잘 자요
Chai jai-yo

When the bright sun has set, up to bed we all go.

We cuddle up close when the moon is aglow.

We all share the same stars that twinkle by night.

We all have our dreams, and we all say,

"Good night!"